This story was inspired by Papa's wisdom
and written for Granny's kidlets:
Xander, Maeve, Beatrice and Daphne
May you always be proud to sing your own song.

Just be who you were created to be!

Liana Ziemer.
2019

Bluebird's Song

By Liana Ziemer

Bluebird could hear a beautiful song, so he landed in a nearby tree to listen to where it was coming from.

Redbird was singing her cheerful morning song.

People were gathering beneath her tree and oohing and aahing and taking her picture while she sang.

Bluebird loved the song and wanted people to love him too, so he opened his mouth to join in the song.

Squawk! Squawk!
OH NO! That didn't work!
The song sounded horrible when Bluebird tried to sing it.

He didn't sound at all like Redbird when he tried to sing her song.

The people turned to Bluebird and told him to be quiet
so they could hear Redbird sing her beautiful song.

They shooed him away!

Bluebird flew away. He was sure he had no talent and nobody loved him.

He hid in a tree and kept very quiet so no one would notice him. Bluebird felt very sad and lonely.

But then he had an idea. AH-HA!

If only he looked more like Redbird, he could sing her song and everyone would love him too.

The next morning he got up early and painted his feathers red and headed out to sing Redbird's song.

Squawk! Squawk!
OH NO! That didn't work!
The song still sounded horrible.

Bluebird wondered if the sounds were coming out all wrong because his beak was a different shape than Redbird's beak.

The next day he got up early, painted his feathers red and attached a new longer beak he had made with cardboard. He was sure this would work.

He perched high on a branch and prepared himself to sing Redbird's beautiful song.

Squawk! Squawk!
OH NO! That didn't work!
The song STILL sounded horrible.

There must be SOMETHING that would work to help him sing like Redbird.

Maybe if he could stand up tall on long thin legs like Redbird, he could reach those beautiful high notes.

He got up early the next morning and painted his feathers red, tied on his long beak and put on his new long legs he had carved from wood.

Squawk! Squawk!
OH NO! That didn't work!
The song STILL sounded horrible!

Bluebird was all out of ideas to help him be more like Redbird so he went home to bed feeling sad.

The next morning, the sunrise was so pretty that Bluebird jumped right out of bed. He forgot to paint his feathers red. He forgot to tie on his long beak. He forgot to attach his long slender legs.

He just gazed at the pretty sunrise and started singing.
Tweet! Tweet! Tweet!
His song sounded so lovely that he just kept on singing.
Tweet! Tweet! Tweet!

Before long, people were gathering beneath his tree to take his picture and record him on their phones.

Bluebird was so happy he found his own beautiful song. And from that day on he sang it every morning because he was proud to be a blue bird.

About the Author

Liana Ziemer lives in Prince George, BC Canada. This is her first book and she credits her late husband, Albert, as being her motivation for fulfilling her longtime dream of becoming an author.

As a musician and worship leader, Albert often encouraged people not to try sing like a redbird if they were a bluebird. Liana has developed this concept into a delightful story for children.

Liana would like to thank Mohsin Khan for the bright and cheerful illustrations he created for this book, and she is grateful for his clever inclusion of a character representing Albert with his signature long goatee, Canada t-shirt and iPhone in hand.

Made in the USA
Columbia, SC
08 August 2019